Lotsa Llama

By Dawn Jones

Illustrated by Steve Pileggi

Cozy Fleece Farm Publishing
Morrison, Colorado

For Emily, who loves llamas and alpacas

Library of Congress Control Number: 2006932465

ISBN 0-9788602-0-9

Printed in United States of America

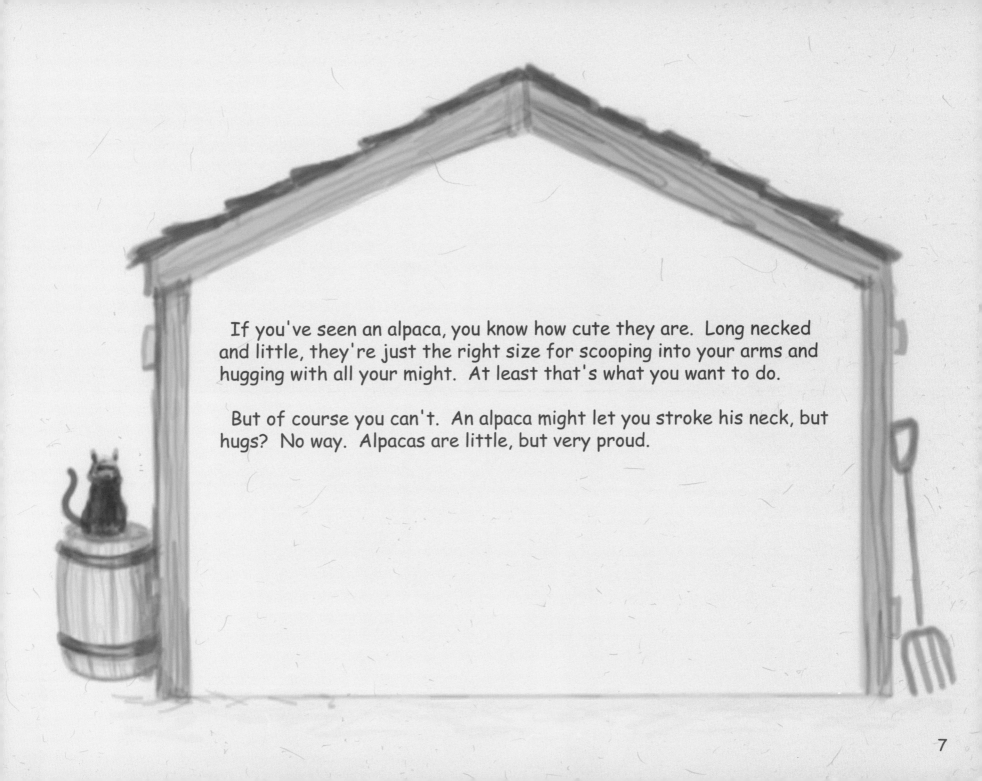

If you've seen an alpaca, you know how cute they are. Long necked and little, they're just the right size for scooping into your arms and hugging with all your might. At least that's what you want to do.

But of course you can't. An alpaca might let you stroke his neck, but hugs? No way. Alpacas are little, but very proud.

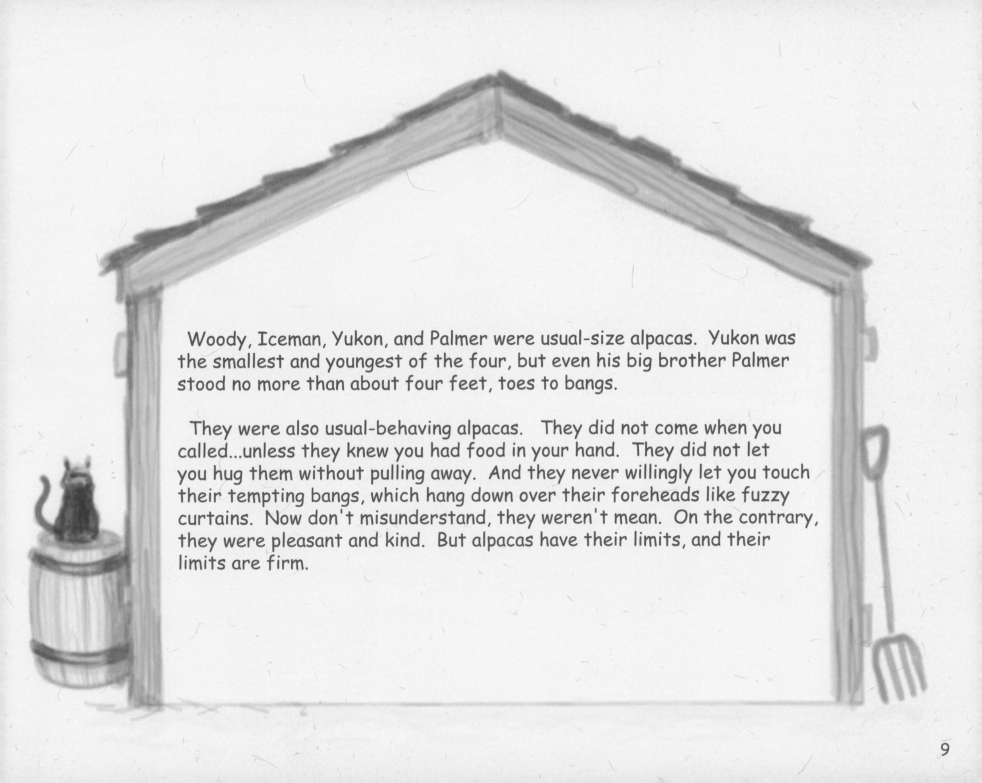

Woody, Iceman, Yukon, and Palmer were usual-size alpacas. Yukon was the smallest and youngest of the four, but even his big brother Palmer stood no more than about four feet, toes to bangs.

They were also usual-behaving alpacas.   They did not come when you called...unless they knew you had food in your hand. They did not let you hug them without pulling away. And they never willingly let you touch their tempting bangs, which hang down over their foreheads like fuzzy curtains. Now don't misunderstand, they weren't mean. On the contrary, they were pleasant and kind. But alpacas have their limits, and their limits are firm.

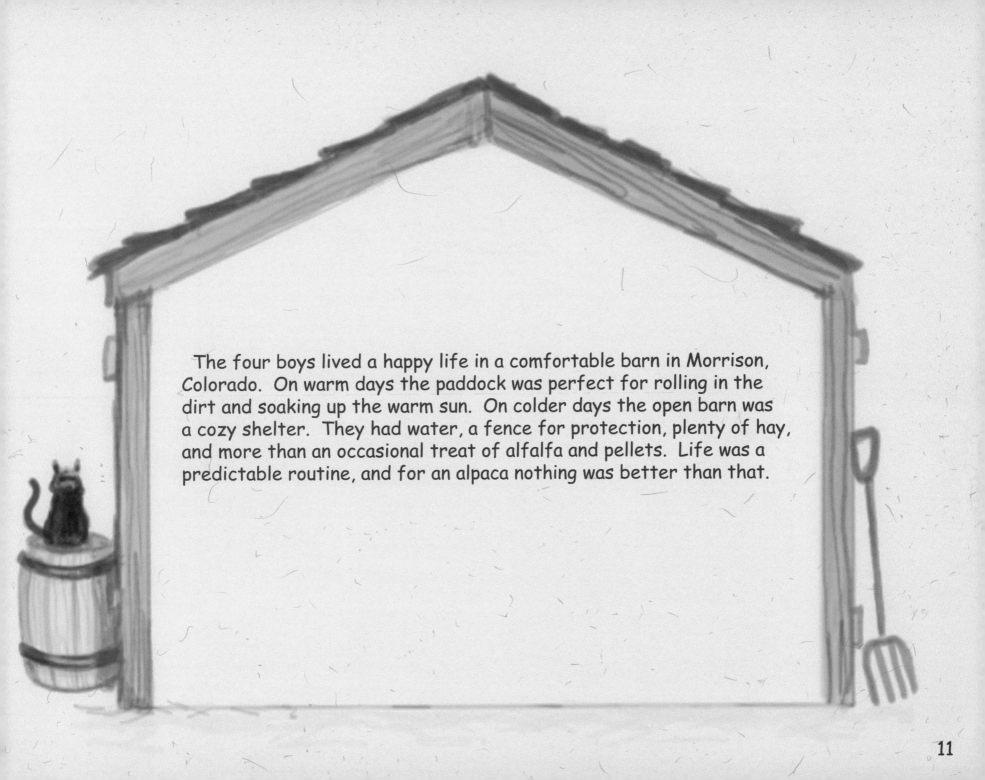

The four boys lived a happy life in a comfortable barn in Morrison, Colorado. On warm days the paddock was perfect for rolling in the dirt and soaking up the warm sun. On colder days the open barn was a cozy shelter. They had water, a fence for protection, plenty of hay, and more than an occasional treat of alfalfa and pellets. Life was a predictable routine, and for an alpaca nothing was better than that.

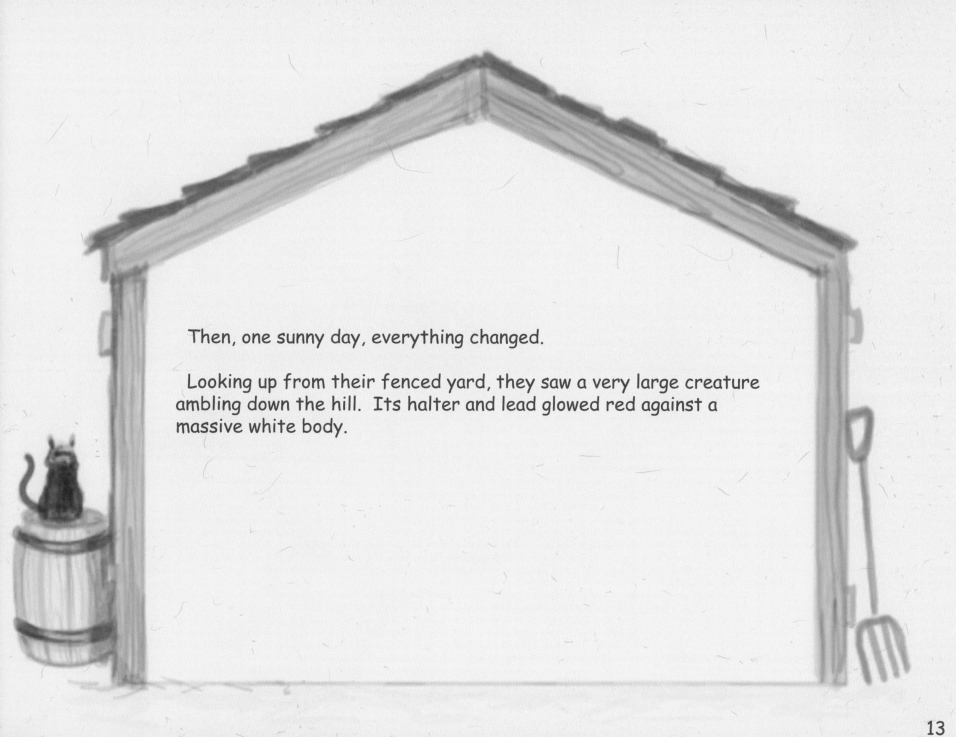

Then, one sunny day, everything changed.

   Looking up from their fenced yard, they saw a very large creature ambling down the hill. Its halter and lead glowed red against a massive white body.

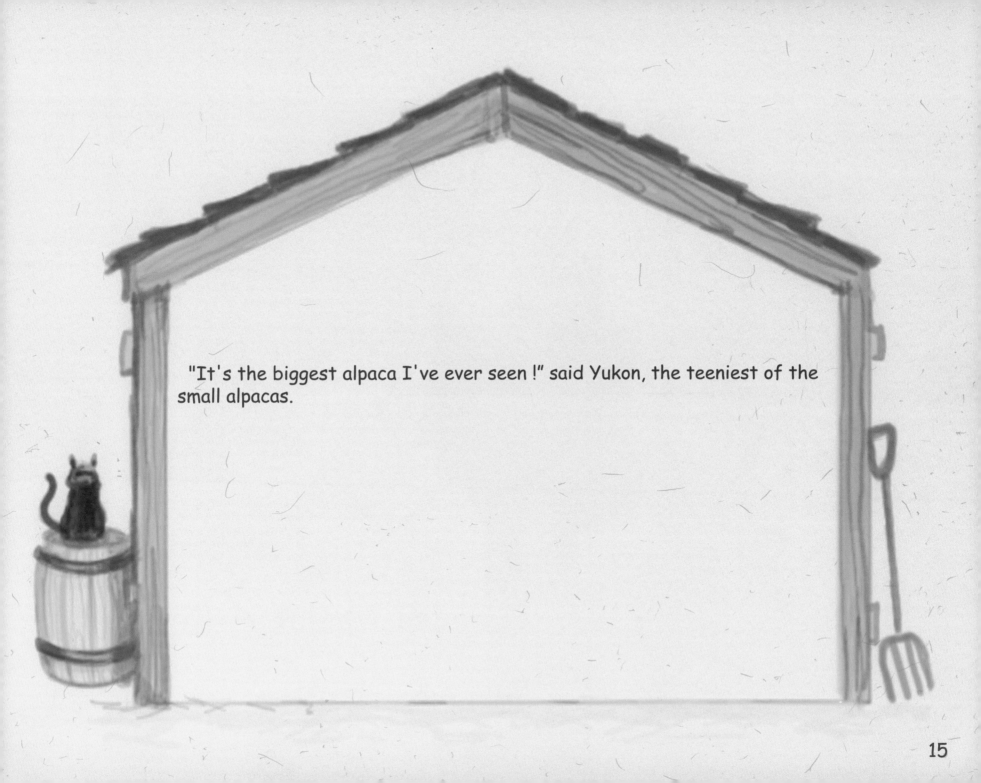

"It's the biggest alpaca I've ever seen !" said Yukon, the teeniest of the small alpacas.

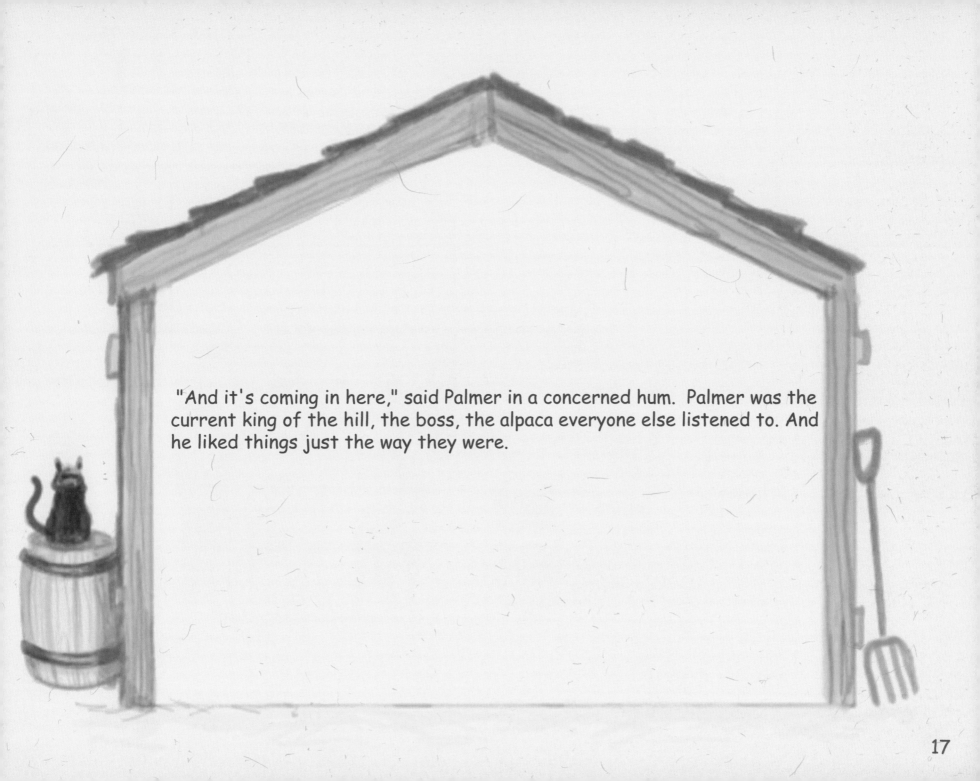

"And it's coming in here," said Palmer in a concerned hum. Palmer was the current king of the hill, the boss, the alpaca everyone else listened to. And he liked things just the way they were.

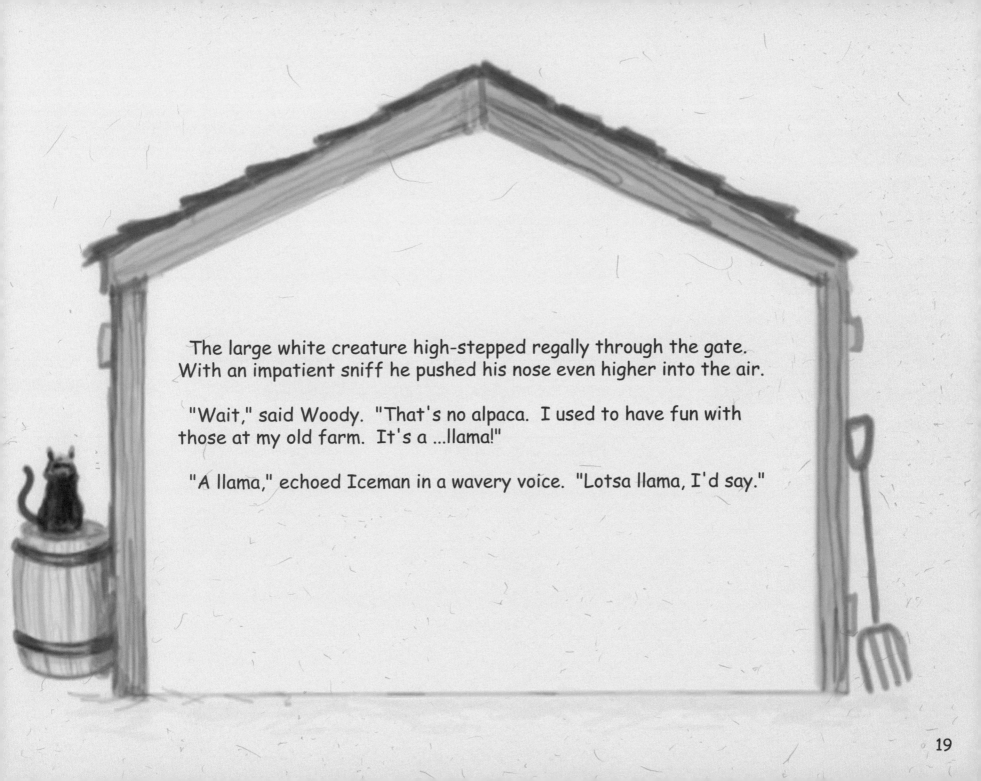

The large white creature high-stepped regally through the gate. With an impatient sniff he pushed his nose even higher into the air.

"Wait," said Woody. "That's no alpaca. I used to have fun with those at my old farm. It's a ...llama!"

"A llama," echoed Iceman in a wavery voice. "Lotsa llama, I'd say."

As the royal white visitor entered their territory all four of them rushed at him like a wave. Hurry, hurry ...they needed to smell him. How else would they know what they were dealing with?

The huge llama flinched, his tail twitching and his body sidling away. But the alpacas didn't give up. Desperate to know more about the new arrival, they crowded around for another whiff as the llama jumped away again. The smelling dance went on for a long time. Finally - somehow - the four little alpacas found out what they needed to know.

The news wasn't good.

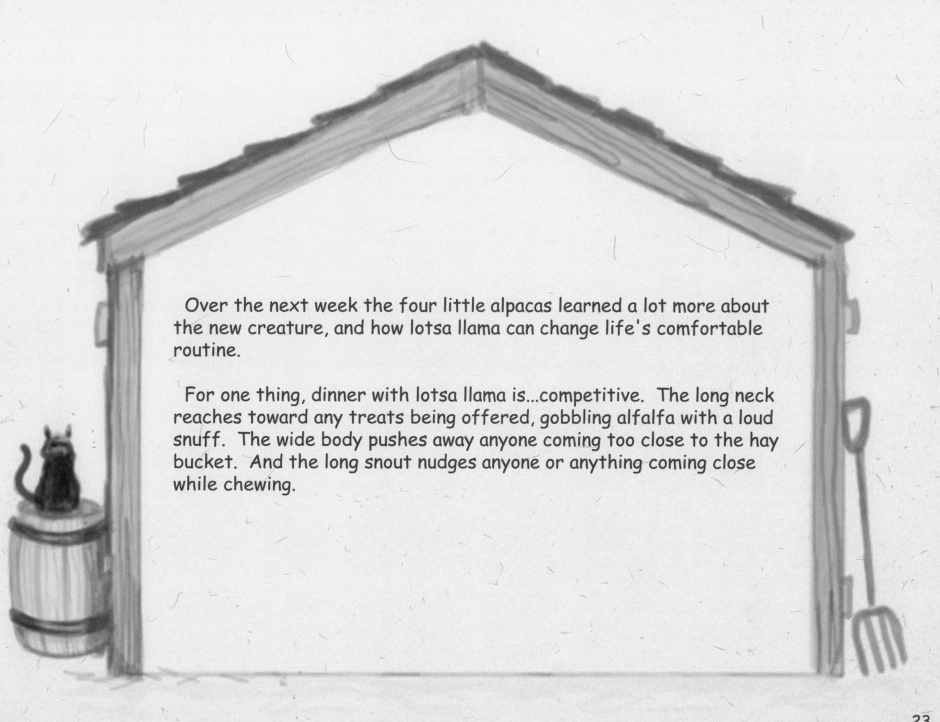

Over the next week the four little alpacas learned a lot more about the new creature, and how lotsa llama can change life's comfortable routine.

For one thing, dinner with lotsa llama is...competitive. The long neck reaches toward any treats being offered, gobbling alfalfa with a loud snuff. The wide body pushes away anyone coming too close to the hay bucket. And the long snout nudges anyone or anything coming close while chewing.

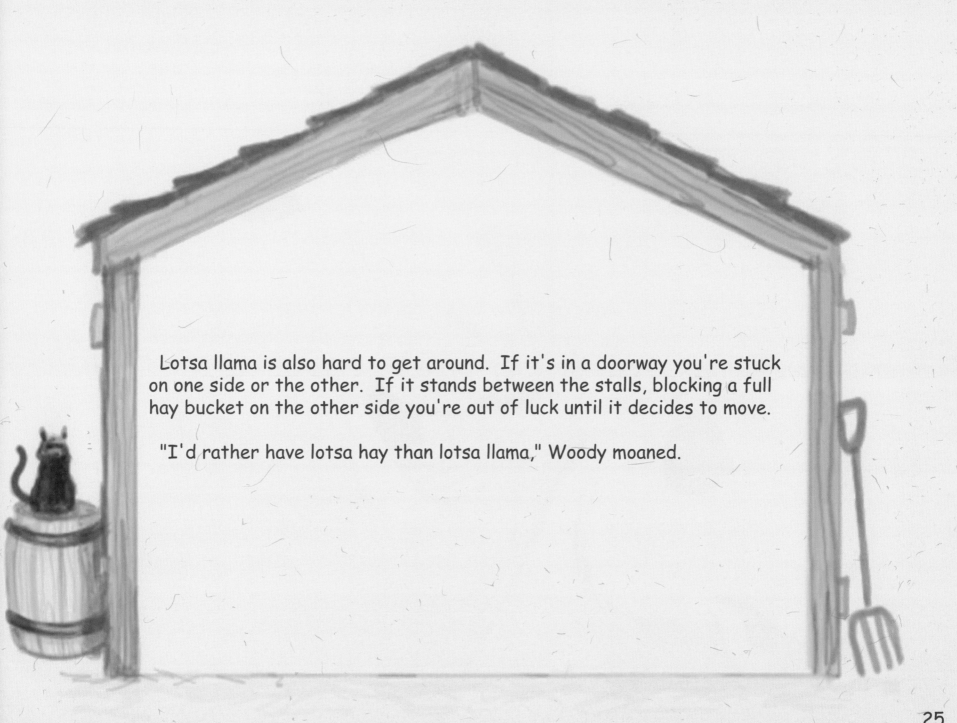

Lotsa llama is also hard to get around. If it's in a doorway you're stuck on one side or the other. If it stands between the stalls, blocking a full hay bucket on the other side you're out of luck until it decides to move.

"I'd rather have lotsa hay than lotsa llama," Woody moaned.

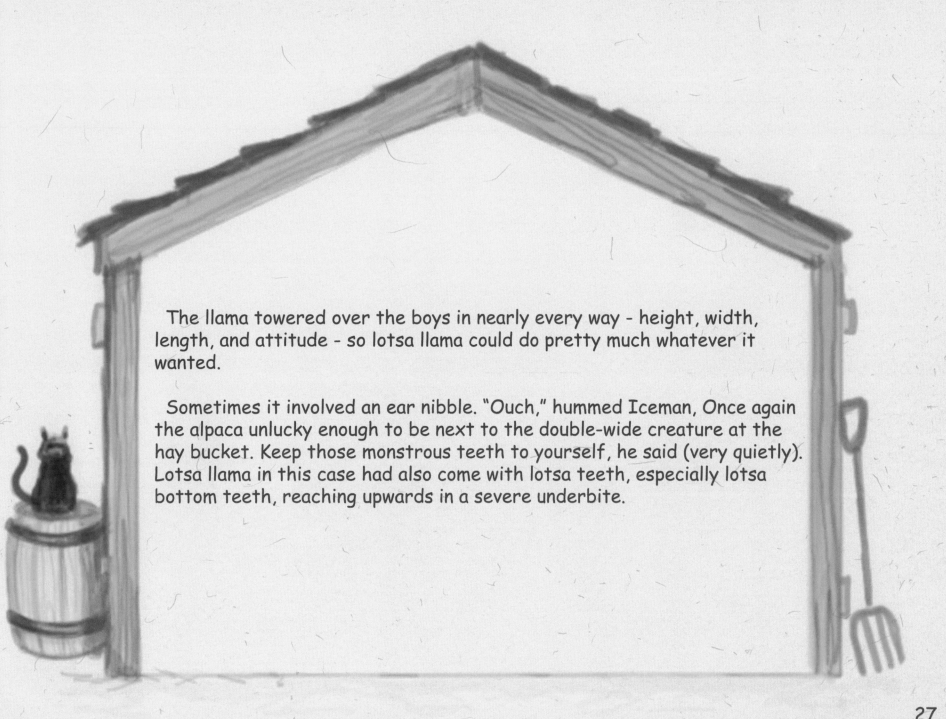

The llama towered over the boys in nearly every way - height, width, length, and attitude - so lotsa llama could do pretty much whatever it wanted.

Sometimes it involved an ear nibble. "Ouch," hummed Iceman, Once again the alpaca unlucky enough to be next to the double-wide creature at the hay bucket. Keep those monstrous teeth to yourself, he said (very quietly). Lotsa llama in this case had also come with lotsa teeth, especially lotsa bottom teeth, reaching upwards in a severe underbite.

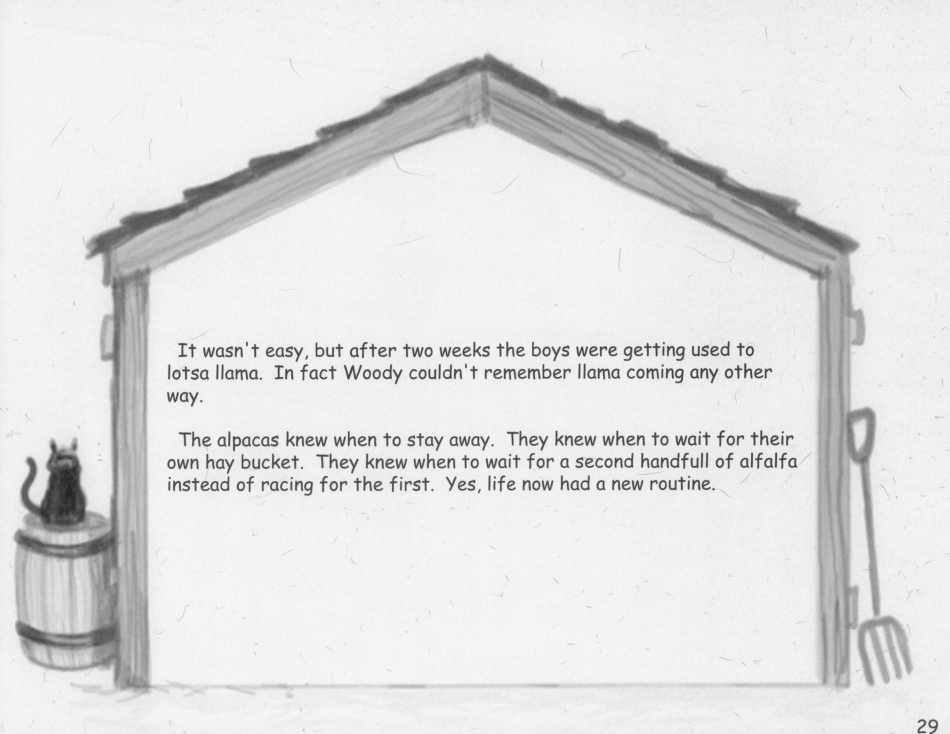

It wasn't easy, but after two weeks the boys were getting used to lotsa llama. In fact Woody couldn't remember llama coming any other way.

The alpacas knew when to stay away. They knew when to wait for their own hay bucket. They knew when to wait for a second handfull of alfalfa instead of racing for the first. Yes, life now had a new routine.

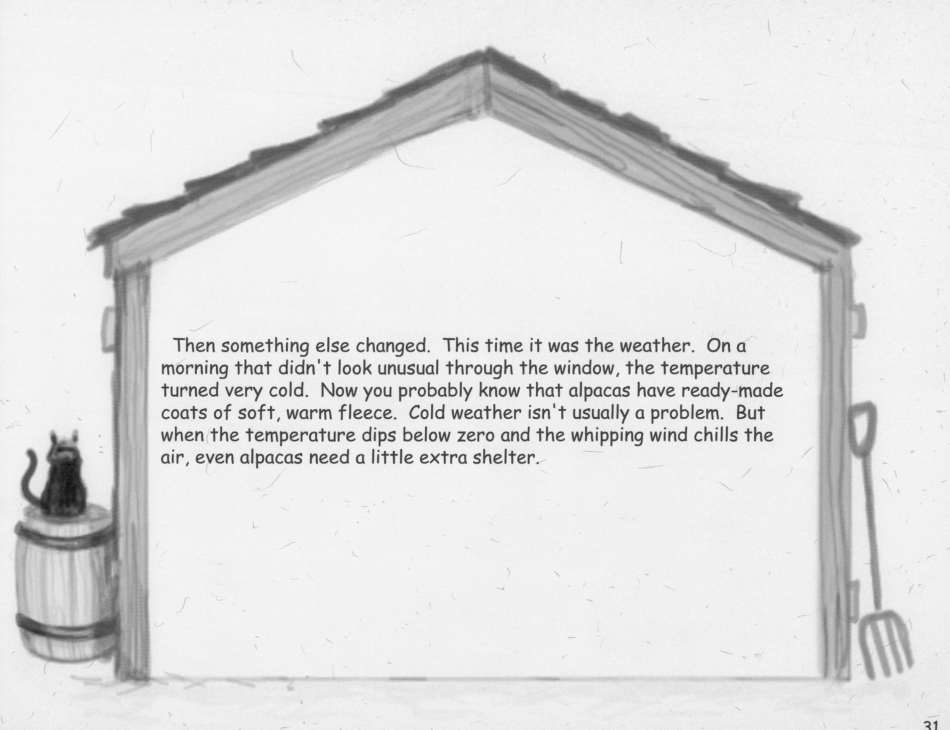

Then something else changed. This time it was the weather. On a morning that didn't look unusual through the window, the temperature turned very cold. Now you probably know that alpacas have ready-made coats of soft, warm fleece. Cold weather isn't usually a problem. But when the temperature dips below zero and the whipping wind chills the air, even alpacas need a little extra shelter.

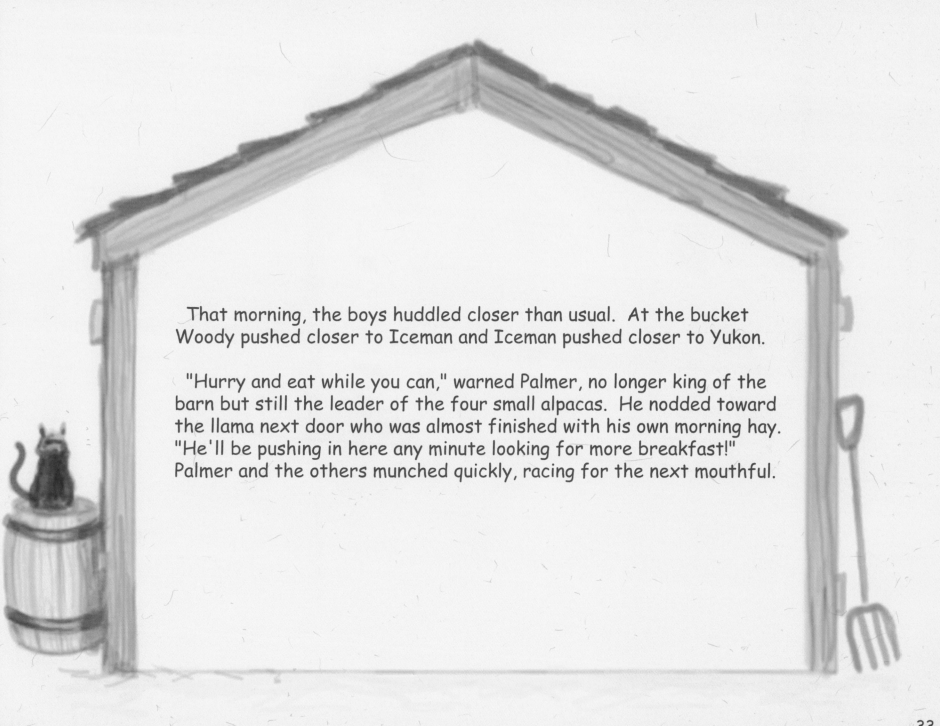

That morning, the boys huddled closer than usual. At the bucket Woody pushed closer to Iceman and Iceman pushed closer to Yukon.

"Hurry and eat while you can," warned Palmer, no longer king of the barn but still the leader of the four small alpacas. He nodded toward the llama next door who was almost finished with his own morning hay. "He'll be pushing in here any minute looking for more breakfast!" Palmer and the others munched quickly, racing for the next mouthful.

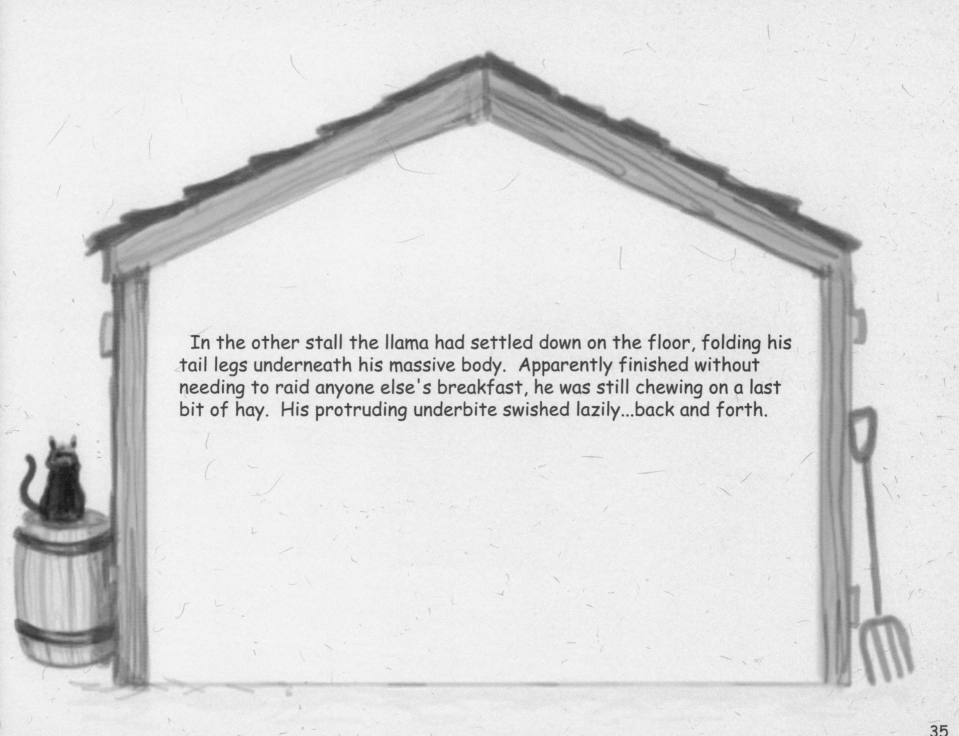

In the other stall the llama had settled down on the floor, folding his tail legs underneath his massive body. Apparently finished without needing to raid anyone else's breakfast, he was still chewing on a last bit of hay. His protruding underbite swished lazily...back and forth.

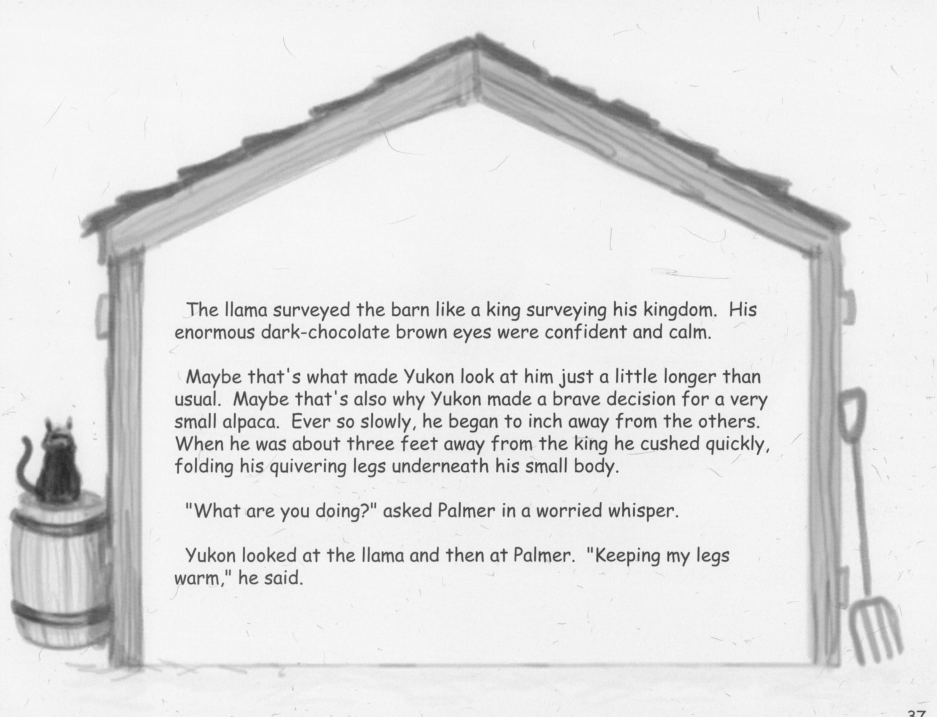

The llama surveyed the barn like a king surveying his kingdom. His enormous dark-chocolate brown eyes were confident and calm.

Maybe that's what made Yukon look at him just a little longer than usual. Maybe that's also why Yukon made a brave decision for a very small alpaca. Ever so slowly, he began to inch away from the others. When he was about three feet away from the king he cushed quickly, folding his quivering legs underneath his small body.

"What are you doing?" asked Palmer in a worried whisper.

Yukon looked at the llama and then at Palmer. "Keeping my legs warm," he said.

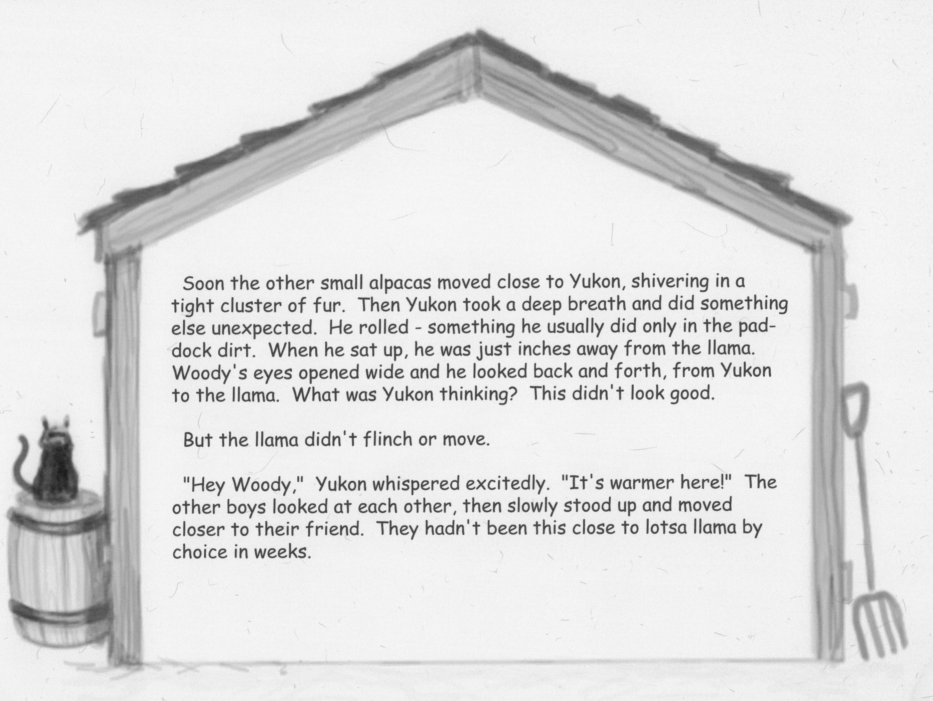

Soon the other small alpacas moved close to Yukon, shivering in a tight cluster of fur. Then Yukon took a deep breath and did something else unexpected. He rolled - something he usually did only in the pad-dock dirt. When he sat up, he was just inches away from the llama. Woody's eyes opened wide and he looked back and forth, from Yukon to the llama. What was Yukon thinking? This didn't look good.

But the llama didn't flinch or move.

"Hey Woody," Yukon whispered excitedly. "It's warmer here!" The other boys looked at each other, then slowly stood up and moved closer to their friend. They hadn't been this close to lotsa llama by choice in weeks.

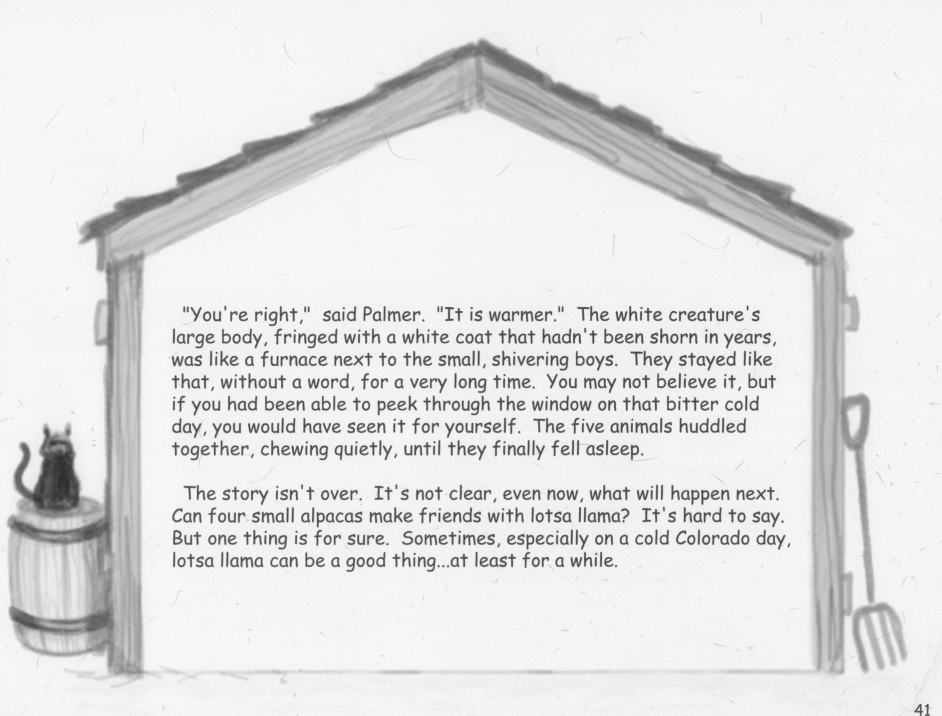

"You're right," said Palmer. "It is warmer." The white creature's large body, fringed with a white coat that hadn't been shorn in years, was like a furnace next to the small, shivering boys. They stayed like that, without a word, for a very long time. You may not believe it, but if you had been able to peek through the window on that bitter cold day, you would have seen it for yourself. The five animals huddled together, chewing quietly, until they finally fell asleep.

The story isn't over. It's not clear, even now, what will happen next. Can four small alpacas make friends with lotsa llama? It's hard to say. But one thing is for sure. Sometimes, especially on a cold Colorado day, lotsa llama can be a good thing...at least for a while.

More About Alpacas

Alpacas and llamas are cousins.
Both are members of the camelid family, which also includes camels, guanacos, and vicuñas. Guanacos and vicuñas still live as wild animals in South America; llamas and alpacas have been domesticated. All camelids have two-toed feet, unlike horses, which have one large toe.

Alpacas eat mostly grass or hay.
Some alpacas eat cut hay; some graze in grassy fields. Many also eat alfalfa as a supplement to the diet. Most alpacas raised on farms or ranches also enjoy pellet chews as a part of their diet. Too many pellets are not good for them, however, and can make them fat. Pellets can sometimes be a choking hazard, too.

There are two kinds of alpacas – Suris and Huacayas.
The alpacas in this story are Huacaya alpacas. Their hair is thick and fleecy like a sheep's wool. Suri alpacas have fleece that hangs from their body in longer ringlets. Both Suris and Huacayas can be found on ranches and farms throughout the United States.

Alpacas love to roll on their backs in the dirt.
Rolling in the dirt seems to open up an alpaca's fleece and releases hay, dirt, and debris, kind of like a bath. It also seems to make them happy.

Alpacas hum.
Humming is the most common sound that alpacas make. Older alpacas usually hum when they are nervous or stressed, for example, when they are separated from herd mates.

To cush means to sit down.
When an alpaca sits down we call it cushing. They fold their legs - opposite to the direction a person's knees fold - and then rest on top. Alpacas often cush when they travel in a van or trailer.

Alpacas are herd animals.
Alpacas need the company of other animals, preferably other alpacas or llamas. Even the short absence of a buddy who's been taken for a walk can make an alpaca feel very stressful.

Alpacas are shorn once a year, usually in spring.
The soft, heavy fleece is very valuable and may weigh anywhere from three to ten pounds or so. After shearing, the fleece is processed to remove impurities such as dirt or hay. It may then be spun into yarn and used to make clothing, or used for felting... or as warm stuffing for quilts and cushions. Alpacas are much cooler for summer without their warm oats, which grow back in plenty of time to keep them warm for winter.

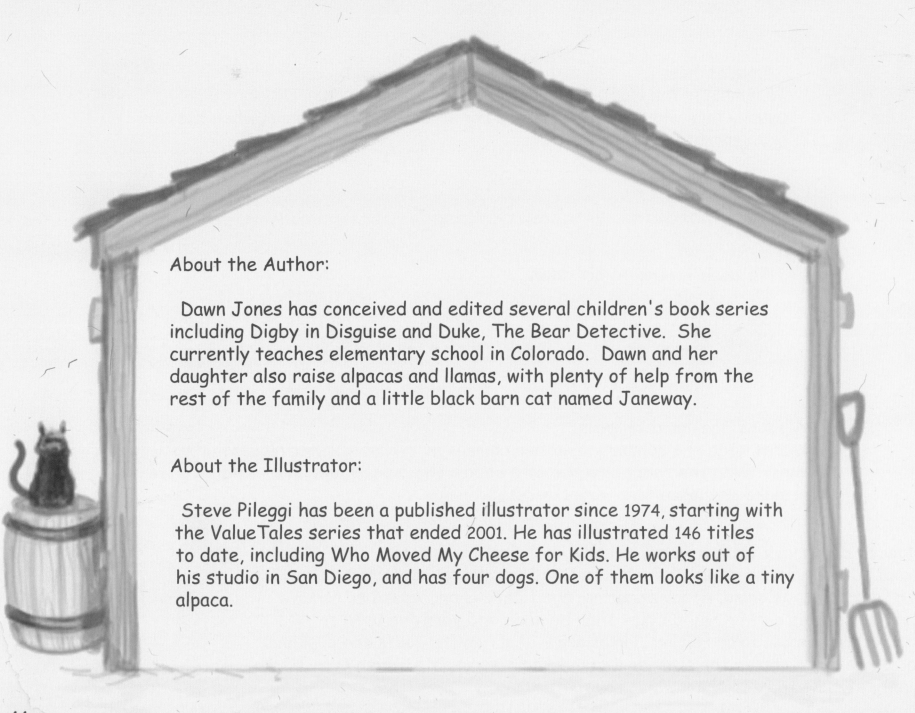

About the Author:

Dawn Jones has conceived and edited several children's book series including Digby in Disguise and Duke, The Bear Detective. She currently teaches elementary school in Colorado. Dawn and her daughter also raise alpacas and llamas, with plenty of help from the rest of the family and a little black barn cat named Janeway.

About the Illustrator:

Steve Pileggi has been a published illustrator since 1974, starting with the ValueTales series that ended 2001. He has illustrated 146 titles to date, including Who Moved My Cheese for Kids. He works out of his studio in San Diego, and has four dogs. One of them looks like a tiny alpaca.